Cypher

The Wonderful Toys

The Wonderful Toys

By *Anna Braune*
with Savilla Sloan

Drawings by
James Graham Hale

HARPER & ROW, PUBLISHERS, NEW YORK
Grand Rapids, Philadelphia, St. Louis, San Francisco
London, Singapore, Sydney, Tokyo, Toronto

Library of Congress Cataloging-in-Publication Data
Braune, Anna.
    The wonderful toys / by Anna Braune : illustrated by James Graham
Hale.
        p.   cm.
    "A Charlotte Zolotow book."
    Summary: Seven toys who have enjoyed a peaceful existence in an
attic trunk are threatened when the owners of the house decide to
clean out the attic.
    ISBN 0-06-020618-7. — ISBN 0-06-020619-5 (lib. bdg.)
    [1. Toys—Fiction.]   I. Hale, James Graham, ill.   II. Title.
PZ7. B7378Wo   1990
[Fic]—dc20

89–77889
CIP
AC

Contents

The Wonderful Toys

Prologue

"Do you mean to say," said Teddy Bear, "that People can't understand anybody but each OTHER?"

"That's right," said the tin alligator.

"Not ANYBODY?" cried White Bunny.

"Not anybody," said the alligator.

"Do you mean to say," White Bunny persisted, "that they can't talk with a bird or a mule or a chair or a tomato?"

"That's what I mean," said Alli.

"Oh, MY," sighed Sheep. "The poor dears."

—*Conversation among toys, overheard*

1
Packing-Away Day

There were seven toys: White Bunny; Cow; Rebecca, who was a doll; Velvi, the black-velvet cat; Teddy Bear; Sheep; and Alli, the tin alligator. They all lived together in a rather unusual dwelling—a trunk. Their companions in the trunk were scraps and rags and worn-out clothes, a cardboard box of straight pins, some mothballs, and Mrs. Mouse and her four children. Since the trunk was home to the toys, they naturally thought of it with a capital *T*. They called the trunk the Trunk.

The Trunk was one of those big, brown, old-timey ones. The lock had been lost out of it a long time ago; so there was now a fairly large, egg-shaped hole where the lock had been. The lock-hole was quite a convenience to everybody in the Trunk, and especially to Alli and Sheep, who lay at the front of the Trunk and near the top. It gave these two some daylight and a small view. And it served as a doorway for the mice. The open lock-hole also made it possible for everybody in the Trunk to hear noises from the outside. Even those down at the very bottom could hear a little bit—when there was anything to hear. There had not been much for a long time.

The Trunk stood in the attic of a very quiet house. There were no children in the house now—only Aunt Essie, a fat aunt, and Aunt Maude, a thin aunt; Tom, who was a cat; and Mr. Mouse. Occasionally Aunt Essie and Aunt Maude came up the stairs and walked past the Trunk, to put something away in the attic or to get something to carry downstairs. Mr. Mouse made trips up and down the stairs, too, to keep Mrs. Mouse and their children supplied with food, but he generally used a little passageway that he knew about inside the wall. Tom, the cat, divided his time between the kitchen and outdoors and was not allowed upstairs at all.

"Something Wonderful is going to happen," said White Bunny.

For a little while none of the other toys spoke. Then the toy cow answered, in a flat, matter-of-fact voice:

"How idiotic."

The Trunk had not been opened for years and years. Cow was thinking of this and of the many days and nights spent in the Trunk by the scraps and rags and worn-out clothes, by the pins and mothballs, by White Bunny, Alli, Rebecca, Sheep, Velvi, Teddy Bear, and herself. She spoke again:

"It does seem idiotic to expect Something Wonderful to happen after we've been shut up in the Trunk so long. Why should it?"

"Why not?" demanded Alli. "It looks to me like it's about time."

"Besides, you can't say nothing ever DID happen," added Teddy Bear. "You can't say it wasn't a big thing, either. A great big thing."

"But you could hardly call it Wonderful," objected Velvi.

Velvi, the black-velvet cat, knew just what Teddy Bear was talking about. They all knew. For Teddy was speaking of the most important—the most upsetting—the most terrific day that they could remember—Packing-Away Day.

Packing-Away Day could never be forgotten. It was on this day, so long ago, that the little girl who called herself their mother—and who was known to them variously as the Child, She, or Her—had gone out of their lives. It was also on this day that Aunt Essie and Aunt Maude had carried the toys up to the attic and packed them away in the Trunk—on top of the scraps and rags and worn-out clothes and pins and moth-balls. *That was the end,* thought Cow, *the beginning of nothing.*

Cow recalled with sadness the very beginning of it all, the Child's departure and farewell. White Bunny, too, was remembering this, but he was remembering with pleasure.

The Child had placed them all in a row against the playroom wall, quite hastily. She was dressed in hat and coat, and the aunts were calling.

"I'm going to Boarding School," She had explained, "where I have to be grown-uppy. So I can't possibly take you with me."

Well, of all things! Velvi, the black-velvet cat, had thought.

Please stay, Cow had begged silently. *Please, please stay.*

"Hurry, dear!" Aunt Essie had called.

"Hurry UP!" Aunt Maude had called.

The Child had not neglected a one of them. Each had been taken in Her arms. "Good-bye— I love you," She had said quickly to each of them.

How hasty, Cow had moaned to herself. *How sadly, sadly hasty.*

White Bunny had been left until last of all. She had not held him for long, only a few seconds longer than the others, really. But Her farewell had been whispered privately in his floppy, slightly soiled ear.

"Good-bye," She had whispered. "I love you.

I love you for keeps, White Bunny. Like a PRES-ENT!"

For KEEPS, White Bunny had thought with joy.

The Child had put White Bunny back in his place in the row of toys and answered the aunts: "I'm coming . . . coming . . . coming!" She had called.

Then She was gone. The toys were alone in the playroom. It had happened so fast.

In no time flat, Alli had thought.

Teddy Bear, who liked to listen for things, had heard the front door open and close. Then all the toys had heard the aunts' familiar footsteps coming up the stairs, and down the hall, past the bedrooms, and toward the playroom. The aunts had come straight in. Aunt Maude had spoken at once.

"It's like I told you, Essie," Aunt Maude had said. "The best thing will be to put them in that trunk. And like I say, the best time to do a thing is NOW."

"But my poor legs!" Aunt Essie had cried. "I TOLD you, Maude, my poor legs don't feel like climbing those attic stairs."

"Who asked your legs?" Aunt Maude had demanded. "Come on, now—you take half and I'll take half."

Half of what? Sheep had wondered.

Half of us, Rebecca had moaned to herself, as if in answer to Sheep's thought. *Oh, my heavens!*

Aunt Maude had picked up Teddy, Cow, and Rebecca and swiftly left the playroom.

"She left me more than half," Aunt Essie had grumbled, but she had lifted each of the remaining toys gently. White Bunny and Velvi were pressed against her soft bosom, and Alli and Sheep were held, right side up, in her free hand. By the time she had climbed the narrow attic stairs, Aunt Maude had the Trunk open and the other three toys inside.

"Toss them in," Aunt Maude had said, "while I get the lamp."

But Aunt Essie had not tossed. While Aunt Maude had moved boxes and chairs to reach the little bedroom lamp, Aunt Essie had arranged the toys as nicely as she could in the Trunk. There was not room to sit them up properly, but at any rate they looked comfortable now, and Cow no longer stood on her head. Aunt Essie had just finished fixing them, with Alli's long nose propped against Sheep's shoulder, when Aunt Maude, lamp in hand, had walked over to the Trunk.

"Let's not stay to PLAY with the toys, Essie," she had said sharply—and pushed the Trunk lid down with a bang.

Like the Bang of Doom, Teddy Bear had thought.

Absolute stillness had followed the bang. Not a toy had spoken a word. The scraps and rags and worn-out clothes and pins and moth-balls—who all sang at night like crickets and katydids—had also been quiet. Velvi, Rebecca, Teddy, and Cow had hated the silence; White Bunny, Alli, and Sheep had scarcely noticed it. White Bunny, indeed, had noticed nothing. He was basking in remembrance of the whispered farewell.

Alli had felt fine. Sheep, of all the toys, was his great favorite—and he was near her. Also, this new independence was to his liking, for he had never enjoyed being carried here and there and goodness knows where, whether he wanted to go or not—even by a nice little thing like Her. Alli had gazed tenderly down his long nose at Sheep's ragged curls. *What luck! Oh, happy, happy landing!*

But no such thoughts had been in Teddy's mind. To him, this was not a happy landing at all. He thought it was awful. *Now I can't see the world go by,* Teddy Bear had grieved. *I can hardly even* HEAR *it!*

Velvi had also felt desperately sad. *Who is there to see me now?* she had moaned. *Who will know that I am velvet?*

Sheep had surprised herself. She, who had never before this moment looked at Alli with any particular interest, had found herself doing so. As she peered sideways at the long, tarnished nose resting upon her shoulder, she had felt oddly contented. *What a long, sweet, intelligent nose,* Sheep had thought.

Suddenly Alli had spoken out loud.

"Now we are on our own," he had said briskly.

But that had been a long time ago.

"Still," said White Bunny, bringing all the toys' thoughts back to the present, "Something Wonderful is going to happen. I feel it."

2
Something Wonderful

"Hush!" cried Velvi. "Look! Listen!"

The toys stopped talking and turned their attention to Mrs. Mouse, who had just stepped out of her nest. They often stopped their conversations while Mrs. Mouse held training sessions with her children, or when Mr. Mouse came through the lock-hole with a feast for his family. The small activities of the Mouse family were of interest to them all, and they now watched and listened as Mrs. Mouse pushed her way toward the central part of the Trunk. *She must be going to see a rag,* thought Cow.

Mrs. Mouse was speaking: "Do you mind if I take a little nibble?" she asked courteously. "May I?" And the rag, a former party blouse made of a soft, soft material called voile, consented at once—just as Mrs. Mouse had felt sure that it would.

All of the rags and scraps and worn-out clothes were generous with Mrs. Mouse. They had gladly shared themselves while she was making the nest for her children; when the children grew bigger, and additions and enlargements were required, they always obliged. Apparently, they enjoyed being useful. And Mrs. Mouse always took only from those who had cloth to spare. Such tiny things as the wee scrap of flannel pajama, soft and tempting as it was, would never be touched. The rags and scraps knew very well that gentle Mrs. Mouse would never, never use one of them all up.

"Certainly, Mrs. Mouse," said the rag who had been a party blouse, "help yourself. But please, dear, do be careful not to bother the tuck. Nor the button." The rag had one tuck and one button.

"Well, that's that," said Velvi as the rag finished speaking. "We might as well talk. She'll be at it for ages. Let's get back to what you said, White Bunny—you know, Something Wonderful."

"I thought that foolishness was all settled," said Cow.

"Is it going to happen to me, White Bunny?" asked Velvi, ignoring Cow. "Is Something Wonderful going to happen to me?"

"Yes," said White Bunny, "to you."

"Something Wonderful for me!" cried Velvi. "A Wonderful of my very own! I'll tell all of you all about my Wonderful. Everything."

"I'll bet," said Alli.

Velvi paid no attention to the interruption. "Here is my Wonderful: I AM JUST LIKE NEW! And I'm where everybody can see me—so pretty, so witty, so kitty (I am a poetess, too, as you can see). And oh, how velvet I am—so very, very velvet. And, of course, I'm greatly admired."

"Of COURSE," Alli agreed.

"Well, my goodness, is she the ONLY one?" cried Teddy. "Don't any of the rest of us have Wonderfuls? How about it, White Bunny?"

"Naturally," said White Bunny.

"Go ahead, Teddy," advised Alli, "before you burst."

But Rebecca interrupted before Teddy Bear could begin. "You'll have to wait, Teddy," said Rebecca firmly, "until White Bunny has had a chance. He really ought to have been first. After all, he started this—or at least he told us about it. Now, White Bunny, tell us about YOUR Wonderful."

Miss Fixit! thought Velvi and Teddy at the same moment.

"Go ahead, White Bunny," prompted Rebecca, "tell it."

"Well, I don't see how I possibly can," said White Bunny slowly, "since I'm in it."

"Good grief!" howled Teddy. "Let ME go on! I assure you that I am NOT in my Wonderful—I am in a Trunk! But I can tell you about it," he said more quietly, "and I can tell you that my Wonderful is a wonderful thing. It is this: TO BE OUT IN THE WORLD ONCE MORE."

Teddy paused briefly. "I guess I'll have to recite it," he said, "like a poem—with sound effects, naturally." And as he began to tell the wonders of the world he loved, his voice did rise and fall in a rich sort of way.

"There go the fire engines—rush-sh-sh-ing and CLANGING and simply TEARING by; that's the train whistle now, that's the old midnight express, going woo-ah, wooo-ah, AH-AH—calling and calling and calling and speeding and speeding away; and oh, the lovely, lovely automobiles! HONK! HONK! HONK! AH-OO-GAH, HONK!" honked Teddy joyously.

"Are you a wild goose or an automobile?" asked Alli.

"How different our Wonderfuls are," said Rebecca dreamily. "Yours is rather mechanical, Teddy; mine is not. Yours is noisy; mine is quiet. Now my Wonderful—"

"Wait a minute!" cried Velvi. "I keep hearing things!"

"Probably just Mrs. Mouse going back to her nest," Rebecca replied crossly. She was eager to tell about her Wonderful.

"Making all THAT racket?" exclaimed Teddy.

"Mrs. Mouse went back long ago. It's the aunts. Come to think of it, they've been tramping around up here for some time."

"It makes me nervous," quavered Velvi, "all that tramping and bumping. Mysterious."

"Nonsense!" said Rebecca sharply. "They are only moving things. Like they do. And as I was saying, IF I may be allowed—here is my Wonderful." Rebecca's voice now became soft and dreamy again. "My Wonderful is a pretty thing. It is where I truly belong. My Wonderful is a WHATNOT."

"A what-WHAT?" asked Teddy.

"A whatNOT," said Rebecca, "which is a lovely little shelf thing where you may sit and sit, along with many pleasant companions, such as Dresden china figurines and little doilies."

"Exciting," Alli remarked sarcastically, "to sit and sit beside a doily."

"I think it could be rather nice," said Sheep uncertainly. As a matter of fact, she was not quite sure whether it WOULD be nice to sit and sit beside a doily, but she wished to be of comfort to Rebecca. "Nearly everyone admires doilies," Sheep went on hurriedly. "They are so pretty.

And they are so very old-timey. Like Rebecca."

Sweet of Sheep, thought Alli tenderly.

"Antique is what I am," said Rebecca stiffly.

"I think I will take my turn," said Cow, "and tell you about my Wonderful. Mine is not a fancy Wonderful, but it is so nice. This is the name of my Wonderful: I belong.

"And this is the way it is," Cow told them, "when my Wonderful comes. Something nice is happening all the time. I am picked up and put down here, and then I am picked up and put down there. Somebody is talking to me and making up answers for me. And everything is playlike: playlike train, playlike house, playlike tea party. Somebody is saying, 'Now then, Cow, you must drink up all your tea. It will make you so nice and warm inside. And it will wash the cookies down!'" Cow stopped. "That is all," she said.

"It sounds like the playroom," said Sheep softly.

"Yes," said Cow.

"I knew it, too," said Velvi.

"We all did," said Alli gently.

But Rebecca had not heard Cow's Wonderful.

Her thoughts were on Alli. She was still angry with him for making fun of the doilies in her Wonderful. *I don't believe he even HAS a Wonderful,* thought Rebecca.

"I think Alli should tell us HIS Wonderful now," said Rebecca, "because he is so CLEVER!"

At first Alli did not reply. How could he? He could hardly tell them that his Wonderful lay right under his nose! Or COULD he? *Why not?* thought Alli mischievously. *They won't know what I'm talking about. I'll get them all mixed up!*

"Well, Alli?" prompted Teddy Bear.

"All right," said Alli, "I'll tell it to you in a riddle:

"My Wonderful is near me,
But does not know it.
My Wonderful is with me,
But has not found out.
What is my Wonderful?"

She's bound to guess, thought Alli dizzily.

Like poetry, thought Sheep. *But what does he mean?*

Only Mrs. Mouse had heard footsteps approaching the Trunk. "Freeze, my darlings," she had whispered to her children. "Freeze!" And she and each little mouse had become utterly still. But the toys had not noticed. By this time they had become so absorbed in their Wonderfuls that all of them, even Velvi, had stopped paying any attention to the noises made by Aunt Essie and Aunt Maude. So the tremendous bump came as a shock.

Something has struck us, thought Cow fearfully. *Maybe the roof of the house!* And indeed something had come down very hard right over their heads, with a great thump that shook the Trunk. But it was not the roof of the house. It was Aunt Essie. Aunt Essie had sat down on the Trunk to rest her legs.

"Get up, Essie," said Aunt Maude. "It's a wonder you didn't cave it in."

"Give me time to rest my legs," begged Aunt Essie. "We have tidied up the whole attic."

"We haven't used soap and water yet," said Aunt Maude, "and we haven't done the trunk. Get up."

"But we NEVER do the trunk!" Aunt Essie objected. "It is full of things." The Trunk creaked as Aunt Essie got up.

Aunt Maude corrected her. "It is full of TRASH," she said, "and we'll get at it tomorrow. Let's go downstairs." The toys listened to their footsteps as Aunt Essie and Aunt Maude went downstairs.

"I didn't know there was any trash in the Trunk," said Sheep. Then she whispered, "Surely, surely she could not have meant the dear little scraps and rags!"

"MORE than the dear little scraps and rags," said Teddy darkly.

"Oh, Teddy," cried Velvi, "what do you mean?"

"Did you say something WONDERFUL was going to happen, White Bunny?" asked Cow pointedly.

"Yes," said White Bunny firmly. "I did."

"Good grief!" groaned Teddy Bear.

Alli had not spoken since Aunt Essie had sat down on the Trunk. But now his voice was heard, comfortingly ordinary, unafraid—and cross:

"I will thank everyone to be quiet," snapped Alli. "I feel nightish."

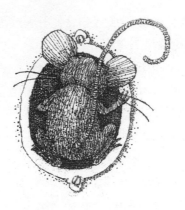

3
Last Peaceful Night

During all the excitement, night had fallen. The lock-hole was dark and the Trunk was quiet. Everything was so peaceful and usual that the toys were now feeling peaceful and usual, too. Aunt Maude's frightening words were fading from their thoughts as bad dreams fade away.

"Something Wonderful," White Bunny began.

"Don't start THAT again," said Velvi. "Listen to the Trunk."

The night sounds of the Trunk were beginning. Like tiny musical instruments tuning up, the straight pins ticked and tinkled in their box. The mothballs were commencing their low, whirring hum.

Like the telephone wires on that country road, thought White Bunny, *when I heard them with Her. When She took me for rides in the car with the aunts.*

A scarlet silk rag, embroidered all over with little rosebuds, lifted its voice:

"I was a gown,
  The talk of the town."

Ah, yes, thought Rebecca, *I saw you.*

Soon all were in full swing. The pins ticked and tinkled all the time. The mothballs constantly hummed. One by one, in little solos, the scraps and rags and worn-out clothes sang remembering songs of their long ago. The Trunk was full of music.

Then there was another sound. A tiny, quick, scratchy sound whispered through the music. Teddy heard it and knew at once that it was

Mr. Mouse. *He has climbed the Trunk,* thought Teddy Bear.

"Mr. Mouse is here," he said aloud, "with the Treasure." And the toys all joined him in watching the lock-hole.

Mr. Mouse would be coming back to the Trunk many times throughout the night, as he brought piece after piece of food for the family feast, but his first visit was always special. Mr. Mouse considered this his pleasure trip. The choice piece of food that he brought now was known to all as the Treasure. And the Treasure was always a gift for Mrs. Mouse alone.

"I am here, my dear!" called Mr. Mouse. "I have the Treasure!" He spoke a little indistinctly, for the Treasure was in his mouth.

Holding firmly to the lock-hole with his two front feet, Mr. Mouse leaned in as far as he could reach and carefully laid the Treasure on top of Alli's head, just between the eyes. It was a crumb of cheese.

Like a jewel, thought Sheep. *How becoming.*

Mrs. Mouse had arrived. For a few moments she was perfectly still, as she gazed lovingly at Mr. Mouse, from head to foot, and saw that he was well. Then she turned her attention to the crumb of cheese on Alli's head. Not a particle of its perfection escaped her. She breathed in its aroma.

"Perfect!" cried Mrs. Mouse. "New enough to be tender; ripe enough to be firm. And the splendid odor! My dear, this is a lovely Treasure."

"It is a small thing," said Mr. Mouse, and he vanished from the lock-hole.

Mrs. Mouse lifted the Treasure from Alli's head.

"But she's not going to eat it!" cried Velvi. "She must have a plan."

Holding it delicately between her teeth, Mrs. Mouse commenced to burrow her way downward through the Trunk. Over and under and between the scraps and rags and worn-out clothes, amongst the humming mothballs, and past the box of tinkling pins she burrowed. Her tongue flicked against the fragrant cheese, but she did not chew. When she reached the very bottom of the Trunk, she pushed her way toward a corner and a heavy scrap of brownish-gold brocade. This was her destination.

"May I put the Treasure beneath you?" asked

Mrs. Mouse courteously. "Will you hide the Treasure and its fragrance?" The brocade consented.

Velvi was the first of the toys to speak after Mrs. Mouse finished hiding the Treasure. Her voice was a little shaky because she was beginning to remember all that had happened during the day.

"I wish she'd exercise the children," said Velvi. "I need to be entertained. Aunt Maude got me all upset."

"What seems to be the trouble?" asked White Bunny.

"Everything," answered Velvi. "Just about everything. I'm worried all over. But I guess it's that Word that bothers me most."

"I wonder—could the Word be TRASH?" Alli inquired loudly.

"Alli!" cried Rebecca. "How horrid of you! Now we will ALL be upset."

I sincerely hope not, thought Alli, and gazed down his nose at Sheep.

Sheep was not in the least upset. *He is brave,* thought Sheep. *He can even say the Word. What a hero!*

28

Cow was talking to Velvi. "Try not to worry so much, Velvi," she was saying. "We will be all right in the Trunk. Nothing is going to happen to us in the Trunk. Nothing ever has."

"I know all that," Velvi agreed, "but there is something else! Suppose," she went on, "suppose—oh, Cow, suppose we are taken OUT!"

"OUT!" cried Teddy instantly. "Splendid! We might see the world!"

"Oh, my goodness!" moaned Velvi miserably. *If only somebody would be scared with me. I'm so lonesome.*

But Velvi was soon to have a small diversion. Mr. Mouse had come back to the lock-hole with a piece of the feast. She watched him as he stood balanced in the lock-hole, swaying a little, holding a long, narrow, limber strip of bacon rind between his teeth. *This will be a little something to entertain me, anyhow,* thought Velvi.

Suddenly a solo began. A worn-out white apron sang its remembering-song:

"Oh, the feasts that I have known!
  They licked their plates and cleaned the bone!"

"Perfectly disgusting!" exclaimed Rebecca. "I certainly never saw such a thing!"

"*I* did," said Teddy, "—pretty nearly, that is. When She used to carry me to the dining room with Her and drop me on the floor by Her chair, I watched them eat. They all ate very well."

"I sat in Her lap," said White Bunny.

"PLEASE!" begged Velvi. "I want to watch Mr. Mouse. He won't stay very long."

It was true. Mr. Mouse never tarried while bringing food for the family feast. The feast had to be ready by dawn, before the aunts were up and about, and he had to gather the food and bring it all to the Trunk. Every inch of the great kitchen spaces must be carefully explored: cabinets, shelves, table, sink, and pantry. Sometimes it was necessary to gnaw through a tough cardboard box. Nearly always some of the food had to be bitten into pieces small enough to carry or drag through the passage in the wall, across the wide attic floor, and up the front of the Trunk. Certainly there was no time for tarrying.

Mr. Mouse turned himself around and backed in through the lock-hole, dragging the bacon rind after him. He was now ready to make his way to the nest, where he and Mrs. Mouse would place the bacon rind on a bare place that she had cleared off for food. It was to be hoped that by dawn there would be a good big pile.

Velvi lost sight of Mr. Mouse when he dragged the rind into the nest, and whatever conversation went on inside was spoken too softly for her to hear. But she was still watching the nest when he reappeared, burrowed his way quickly to the lock-hole, and dropped lightly to the attic floor. *I enjoyed that,* she thought, and realized that she was feeling better. In a moment, she also realized that the other toys were talking.

"And perhaps we WON'T be taken out," Rebecca was saying. "Perhaps, instead, something will be put IN."

"You're dreaming," observed Cow.

"No, really," Rebecca insisted, "it might happen. There's plenty of room on top. Things COULD be put in."

"What, for instance?" asked Teddy Bear.

"Need you ask?" Alli inquired. "Have you forgotten so soon? Doilies, of course."

"Linens," said Rebecca. "Lovely, lovely linens

for the table." Her voice had softened. "There's room for many folded linens," she went on, "and they could lie right on top of us. Now what could be pleasanter than to lie beneath the lovely linens?"

"I could name you a list," offered Alli.

Before Rebecca had time to reply, or even grow angry, it happened. Teddy was the first to see it, and his voice rang out through the Trunk:

"Here she COMES!"

The thing they had all been waiting for was commencing. Velvi's wish was coming true. Mrs. Mouse was emerging from the nest—followed by her four children.

"She's going to EXERCISE them!" cried Velvi.

Mrs. Mouse led the children around White Bunny, over Rebecca, and toward the shiny scrap of blue satin that was the exercise arena. The children followed just behind her, exactly in the order of their names. The largest one, known as The Swiftest, was at her heels. Close behind The Swiftest came Fast and Medium Fast, the sisters. The smallest mouse, Slow, came last of all. He followed about two inches behind the others. When they had all reached the blue-satin exercise arena, the children commenced a wild, scampering game of chase. Mrs. Mouse settled herself comfortably at the edge of the arena, propped against Teddy Bear's foot.

"Halt! Attention!" called Mrs. Mouse.

Each of the children slid to a stop on the shiny blue satin and stood motionless.

Like a game of Still-Statue-No-More-Moving, thought White Bunny.

"Our first game will be Follow the Leader," Mrs. Mouse told them. "The Swiftest will lead, then Fast, Medium Fast, and Slow. Line up now—and go!"

They were off! Almost faster than the toys could see, The Swiftest led the other three. Up Sheep's side, down Alli's nose—between the toys, over them, under them—burrowing, sliding, racing—up, down, over. On and on they streaked through the Trunk until, suddenly, Mrs. Mouse called out.

"On base!"

Instantly, The Swiftest, Fast, and Medium Fast skimmed up Teddy's side and flew in an arc from the tip of his nose to the shiny satin arena. They landed in a little heap beside Mrs. Mouse. It took Slow only seconds longer to follow their path—over Velvi, up Teddy Bear, and off the end of his nose. But he was late. He landed on the blue satin alone.

"You made it, my boy," said Teddy Bear quietly.

"Now for the Contest!" Mrs. Mouse called out, and the four children gathered around her to listen.

"The Contest will test the power of your noses," Mrs. Mouse told them. "Very important. There will be a prize for the winner, which is hidden. The winner must find it."

The little mice crouched, ready to spring off for the hunt. But Mrs. Mouse was not quite ready to let them go.

"Listen quietly," she said, "and let me tell you about the prize—which is very well hidden. You will have to trace it by its scent, through all the smells of the Trunk: cloth, sawdust, mothballs, and the smell of the Trunk itself. This will not be easy. But the reward, my dears, is great. The prize is indeed of value—the finest crumb of cheese in the world! . . . It is the Treasure," she finished softly, and gave them leave to start.

"Well, for goodness' sake," exclaimed Velvi, "so that's it! She's turned the Treasure into the prize."

"Look at Slow," said Rebecca. "He's just sitting there."

It was true. Slow was sitting perfectly still while the other three burrowed rapidly about, sniffing and searching. For several seconds he remained motionless, except for his twitching nose.

"I think he's going to win," said Teddy Bear.

Slow was changing position. Very slowly he raised himself upright, straighter and straighter and higher, until he stood like an arrow, his nose pointing toward the roof of the Trunk. Suddenly, he dropped to his four feet and burrowed downward.

Medium Fast, Fast, and The Swiftest were still searching and sniffing while Slow worked his way from the scrap of brownish-gold brocade toward the top of the Trunk. The crumb of cheese was held carefully between his teeth. When he reached the top, he crossed the blue-satin arena and laid the Treasure at Mrs. Mouse's feet.

"You have won!" cried Mrs. Mouse. "My dear, you may eat it."

"I don't want it," said Slow. "It's yours."

Mrs. Mouse looked gratefully at Slow and lifted the crumb of cheese. For a long moment, she held it in her mouth. Then she chewed.

Fast, Medium Fast, and The Swiftest had already given up and started for the arena when Mrs. Mouse called them.

"Come back, all! The exercises are over. Now we will dance!"

At Mrs. Mouse's words, the pins and mothballs began to tinkle and hum with such gaiety that their music seemed to sparkle through the Trunk. Scraps and rags and worn-out clothes sang without pause in an unending succession of solos. The little mice ran to the center of the blue-satin arena, while Mrs. Mouse settled herself comfortably against Teddy Bear's foot. The toys looked on with joy.

"Oh, my goodness!" cried Velvi happily.

"The music is for Mrs. Mouse," said Cow.

"It's a great big grand PRESENT for her," shouted Teddy Bear, "from the scraps and rags and worn-out clothes and pins and mothballs!"

"But I can hear it, too!" cried Velvi. "That makes it mine, too!"

"Of course it is, Velvi," said White Bunny.

And the little mice danced. The Swiftest simply flew into the wildest and most exciting airs, leaping and whirling and slashing about with his tail. Slow moved with flowing grace through waltzes and gentle lullabies. Fast and Medium Fast danced at medium speed, in perfect time, to every song as it came along. Together they sailed around and around the shiny blue-satin arena—skimming, swaying, gliding.

But it was soon to end. Scarcely noticeably at first, the music slowed. The tick and hum of pins and mothballs was becoming very faint. Solos came only at intervals, and as though from far away. At a signal, Mrs. Mouse's children lined up behind her. Then, still on tiptoe and lightly skipping, they followed their mother across the blue arena, around the toys, and toward the nest. The Trunk was silent.

"Here's Mr. Mouse," whispered Teddy. "He has come to the feast!"

"Then it's dawn," said Velvi.

Quiet settled on the Trunk save for smothered murmurs from the mouse nest. Even those ended when Mr. Mouse reappeared, climbed up to the lock-hole, bowed his head in a quick good-bye, and disappeared from sight.

4
Prepare!

Just as the shaft of sunlight that streamed through the lock-hole struck the tarnish and flaking paint on the top of Alli's head and turned it to a dazzling blaze of lovely color—and Sheep felt that she would burst with admiration—the toys heard the aunts come back to the attic. Then, almost at once, they heard cleaning-up noises.

"They are doing it with soap and water," said

Velvi, "just like Aunt Maude said they would."

"Yes," Teddy agreed, "I heard water splashing and sloshing when the mop was being slopped around in the bucket. Afterward, when the water simply poured, I knew somebody was wringing out the mop. And listen now! The mop is pushing and pushing over the attic floor."

Rebecca corrected him. "BEING pushed," she told him firmly. "And you needn't bother to explain things, either. We know." She had intended to remind Teddy of how often they had all watched, many and many a time, while the playroom was being cleaned up and mopped. But she stopped quickly when Aunt Maude began to speak.

"Hand me the mop, Essie—you're too slow. You can wipe things off with this damp cloth while I mop. And leave the soap in the water so the water will be good and soapy."

"It will get soft," said Aunt Essie. "The soap, I mean."

Aunt Maude must not have cared; she did not answer.

"I've been thinking and thinking," said Sheep, "but I can't think of a word for that noise. What's a word for the noise the mop makes? Somebody tell me."

"Sloopy?" suggested Alli.

"Of course," murmured Sheep. "Thank you."

"Don't thank him!" cried Rebecca. "SLOOPY! What a horrid, wet word! Like the mop had not been wrung out at all. Now I would say the mop makes a WHISPERY sound."

"I'd say WHOOSHY!" shouted Teddy Bear, as Aunt Maude swooped past the Trunk with the mop.

"Well, I'd say what a tiresome conversation," complained Cow, "and what a tiresome TIME. I think they are going to mop and wipe things off forever."

"I don't think so," said Alli. "Cleaning up was only the first half of Aunt Maude's plan. Remember?"

"Don't, Alli, don't," pleaded Velvi. "I don't want to remember the other half." And immediately she commenced to remember.

But the cleaning-up noises went on and on until late in the day.

"Everything seems very quiet all of a sudden," said Sheep.

The sound of mopping had stopped. Not a whisper came through the lock-hole. Aunt Maude's voice was startling as it rose in the quietness, calling to Aunt Essie across the attic room:

"Essie! We can do it now, Essie. We can do the trunk. You open it while I finish wiping things off."

Aunt Essie opened the Trunk.

Light and sound burst upon the toys. In a flash, they were drenched in dazzling late-afternoon light; they were in the midst of a jumble of noise.

It's a regular blaze, thought Alli, *and what a racket!*

Teddy Bear immediately busied himself with sorting out different noises. Listening carefully, he recognized several: a bird called to an answering bird; from far away a dog barked, and another, from farther still, barked back; a wasp buzzed and thumped as it sailed high above the Trunk, bumping itself against the attic rafters. Teddy listened to each with a small prick of pleasure and recognition. But over them all, and all the time, he was hearing the most beautiful noises

of all—the sounds of motors from the street below, and the honking horns.

So far, so glorious, thought Teddy Bear. *So
far, so* VERY *glorious!*

Aunt Maude called out impatiently:

"What are you doing, Essie?"

Aunt Essie was standing quite still beside the
open Trunk. A little smile lifted the corners of
her mouth as she looked down upon the toys:
Velvi, Cow, Rebecca, Teddy, White Bunny, and
Alli, with his nose propped against Sheep's side.

"The toys look sweet," said Aunt Essie softly.
"They are just like I fixed them."

"Did you expect them to get up and rearrange
themselves?" asked Aunt Maude. "For goodness'
sake, Essie, get those things out of the trunk!"

But Aunt Essie did not budge. Something
queer seemed to have happened to her. She stood
as though frozen. The little smile had vanished
from her face, and she was staring with horror
into the open Trunk.

"Maude!" she cried. "Maude! Come here at
once! The trunk is MOVING! At least SOMETHING
is moving!"

Aunt Maude was beside her in an instant,

peering down at the toys and scraps and rags and worn-out clothes that surrounded them. All was motionless.

"But they DID move, Maude," Aunt Essie insisted in a high-pitched, quavery voice. "They did! Those rags right there, Maude—they quivered, I tell you! Or perhaps they heaved up a little. It's those right there!" She pointed to the rags that were the roof of Mrs. Mouse's nest.

Aunt Maude looked up from the Trunk to Aunt Essie's face. "Do you feel well, Essie?" she inquired.

"Look CLOSELY!" Aunt Essie begged her. "I implore you!"

"I suppose I'll have to," said Aunt Maude, and obliged.

She leaned far into the Trunk, looking carefully at the rags that Aunt Essie had pointed out. She leaned in so far that the tip of her nose almost touched the roof of the nest. Then she jumped back and slammed down the lid with a shattering crash.

Inside the Trunk, not a word was spoken. None of the toys felt able to speak.

"MICE!" screamed Aunt Maude. "I smelled

mice!" Her voice rang through the lock-hole loud and clear.

"Well!" exclaimed Aunt Essie. "Is THAT all it was?" Aunt Essie's voice sounded relieved, almost happy.

"The smell was very STRONG," Aunt Maude went on. "Essie, that trunk is probably full of mice."

"Shall we let them out?" asked Aunt Essie.

"Really, Essie!" said Aunt Maude.

"What are you going to do, Maude?" asked Essie. She sounded worried.

"I'm going to bring Tom up tomorrow morning," said Aunt Maude, "just as soon as he comes in for his breakfast. And right now I'm going to stop up that lock-hole. Hand me the soap."

"But they won't be able to get out," Aunt Essie objected.

"Let's hope not," said Aunt Maude.

The lock-hole was suddenly black. Aunt Maude had pressed the damp soap in so well that the opening was completely filled.

"Good gracious!" cried Cow.

"Now we can't hear ANYTHING," said Teddy Bear miserably.

"You can if you listen hard," said Velvi.

All of them listened hard. They could barely hear Aunt Maude's muffled voice declare with satisfaction: "It's been a good day's work, Essie," and Aunt Essie's plaintive reply: "It's been a LONG day's work, Maude. My legs tell me so." The aunts' footsteps sounded fainter and fainter and then ceased altogether.

"Isn't Tom the cat?" asked Sheep, whispering so the mice wouldn't hear. "The cat Mr. Mouse is always talking about?"

"I'm afraid so," answered Alli.

All the toys were silent for a few moments. Then Velvi spoke. "I am not like Tom," she said softly. "I am a different kind of cat. In lots of ways."

"Of course, you are," Alli told her, and his voice was gentle. "We all know it, Velvi. After all, you are velvet."

"That's just what I was thinking," said Velvi.

With one accord, the toys all looked at the nest. Mrs. Mouse stood in the entrance, staring toward the lock-hole. Her nose was twitching and her eyes were very wide. After glancing fearfully this way and that, as though danger might lurk within the Trunk itself, she jumped from the nest and hurried to the exercise arena. She seemed quite distracted.

Maybe she'll begin to feel better after she takes a little rest by my foot, thought Teddy.

But Mrs. Mouse did not rest. She did not settle herself comfortably against Teddy Bear's foot, as was her usual custom. Instead, she ran aimlessly about in the blue-satin arena, zigzagging from edge to edge, talking to herself.

"Mr. Mouse will manage," she told herself firmly. "Of course he will be able to release us. Of course! Of course! OF COURSE!"

I'm trying to believe it, thought Sheep.

"I fear for you, Mrs. Mouse," said Cow softly.

But Mrs. Mouse was regaining her confidence. "I must plan," she said calmly. Her voice was almost businesslike.

Mrs. Mouse now walked slowly and deliberately around the edge of the arena, her head lowered in thought. Now and then she expressed her thoughts aloud, as if to fasten them in her mind.

"The children must be absolutely ready," said Mrs. Mouse. "They must be prepared. They must be drilled." She walked around the arena.

I wish she'd say it ALL *out loud,* thought Velvi, *so we'd know what's going to happen. I'm tired of mysteries and surprises.*

"Yes," said Mrs. Mouse, "I will have to line them up. And, more than that, they will have to be lined up PROPERLY—or there will be a terrible calamity!" She walked around the edge of the arena. "What about Slow?" she whispered.

She's worried about him, thought Teddy Bear uneasily. *She doesn't know what to do with him. And no wonder! Everything takes Slow forever.*

Mrs. Mouse walked slowly and silently around the edge of the arena three times more, and then she spoke. This time her voice was loud and sure.

"Why, of course!" she cried. "Now I have it! Slow will be at the HEAD of the line—with all the others behind him. He will be PUSHED through the lock-hole. The Swiftest will be at the very end—and his magnificent strength will send them flying! The middle of the line doesn't matter."

Mrs. Mouse called her children.

5
The Strange and Exciting Hours

The instant the little ones scampered onto the arena, she called them to order and led them straight to the slab of soap that blocked up the lock-hole. Each of them was asked to examine it carefully, and to touch it. Then, while all stood close to the sticky, slimy soap, she told them about the awful task that awaited their father.

"Now think of it!" cried Mrs. Mouse. "He'll have to gnaw through that awful stuff. Just think of such bravery, my dears!

"You must remember EVERYTHING, my dears," Mrs. Mouse told her children. "Always remember to face the lock-hole while standing in line. Slow, do not forget that little rip in the arena floor, which is your battle station. And all of you must be sure, sure, SURE to remember the two words of command."

"For— For— Formation," whispered Slow, "and Charge . . . Charge . . . Charge."

He knows both of those words, thought Teddy Bear with relief. *Thank goodness for that!*

After some rehearsing, Mrs. Mouse announced: "That is all; it is time now to wait. Never stop remembering. Now you may go."

The little mice crept to the nest.

"How long has it been night?" asked Sheep.

Nobody knew. None of the toys could be sure how long ago night had fallen. They had been too much absorbed in the activities of Mrs. Mouse and her children to listen for the sounds that heralded night in the Trunk. Only after Mrs. Mouse had sent the little ones back to the nest, and it was silent, did the toys become aware of other sounds. When they heard them, the toys were amazed.

"I should think we would have heard this no matter WHAT else was going on," declared Teddy Bear.

Cow agreed. "The sounds are PECULIAR," she added in a low, gloomy voice.

"They aren't even MUSIC anymore!" cried Velvi.

Cow and Velvi were both right. Scratchy, scrapy whines had replaced the melodious hum of mothballs. Only an occasional dismal click sounded in the box where straight pins had so joyously tinkled. Scraps and rags and worn-out clothes had all given up using words when they sang. Their melancholy voices rose and fell in the Trunk.

"Aa—aahh," wailed a rag.

"Aa—aaahh," echoed scraps and worn-out clothes.

"Good gracious!" cried Velvi.

I'm not easily saddened, thought Teddy Bear, *but this seems to be a little too much for me.*

"I don't understand," Sheep quavered. "What

do all these curious noises mean? WHY?" she asked unhappily. "WHAT?"

"Signs of the times, I would say," said Alli. "SOUNDS of the times, that is."

I knew he could explain, thought Sheep, comforted.

He's a horrid, discouraging thing, Cow thought, *but I do believe he is right. All these noises do sound exactly like right now!*

"We mustn't give up hope," said White Bunny.

"Why should I hope?" Cow asked in a loud, sad voice.

Suddenly then, and as though in answer to Cow's question, a familiar line of the Dreamland Song rang out in the Trunk—in words!

"You might land in the lollipop tree!" sang the old pillowcase cheerfully.

"Very likely!" scoffed Rebecca.

"Well, now, it COULD be very likely," said White Bunny. "Why not?"

"Yes, yes!" exclaimed Teddy enthusiastically. "Certainly! A very good idea! Everything COULD end well, you know. Everything could end in OUT!"

"Out WHERE, may I ask?" inquired Cow.

"Ah—aaahh," wailed a rag.

"Out where Mr. Mouse is, maybe," suggested Velvi, "wherever that is. I wish he'd hurry up and come."

"He probably won't," said Rebecca. "He probably doesn't see any reason why he should. For all he knows, everything is just fine in here. He may not come for ages and ages."

Cow spoke quickly: "I beg to differ with you, Rebecca. If you will recall, Mr. Mouse is in the habit of bringing the Treasure quite early each evening. He should be here soon—any minute now."

They all looked toward Mrs. Mouse, who sat hunched in the middle of the arena, staring at the lock-hole.

"She hasn't rested at all," said Teddy Bear in a worried voice. "She has only waited."

Mrs. Mouse stirred. As the toys watched, she changed position, arose, and sat upright, very straight and alert.

"She hears something!" cried Teddy Bear. "And so do I! Listen!"

Mr. Mouse's voice could be heard, ever so faintly, calling from the attic floor.

"I am here. I have the Treasure."

Mrs. Mouse moved closer to the lock-hole. "Mr. Mouse!" she shouted. "Can you hear me?"

Mr. Mouse called again. "Answer me, my dear! Come to the lock-hole."

Surely he will come up the Trunk, thought Teddy Bear. *Surely her silence will tell him that something queer is going on!*

Mr. Mouse's voice came sifting through the lock-hole in a faint, faraway shout:

"It is CAKE! Very fresh . . . with ICING! CHOC-OLATE!"

"Oh, my very dear," breathed Mrs. Mouse, "what a lovely, lovely Treasure you have brought me! And however did you manage? Up the long steep passageway and across the enormous floor —and with the icing still on!" She raised her face up toward the lock-hole. "No matter!" she called loudly and sternly. "DROP IT!"

"Yes, indeed," replied Mr. Mouse gaily, "that is EXACTLY what I said: CHOCOLATE!"

Dear me! thought Rebecca nervously. *He might as well be stone deaf!*

Mrs. Mouse tried again. "LEAVE it!" she yelled. "Come HERE! I NEED you!"

This time Mr. Mouse heard correctly. She

needed him! Tossing the Treasure aside, he started up the front of the Trunk. He did not notice that the delicate cake crumbled as it struck the floor.

The toys had all listened intently while Mr. Mouse's toenails made little scratchy sounds as he ascended the Trunk. Now they waited for his encounter with the closed lock-hole. What would be his exclamation, what his outcry, when he came face to face with the slimy soap? They waited in strained silence.

He will probably yell, thought Teddy Bear. *This is certainly a yelling matter.*

But he did not yell; there was no outcry. After Mr. Mouse's toenails stopped scratching against the Trunk, the Trunk was silent.

"He is overcome," whispered Rebecca.

An anxious Mrs. Mouse arose immediately from where she was crouched by the soap and commenced to move about. With frequent glances toward the lock-hole, she walked back and forth across the arena and around and over toys until, finally, she came to a stop beside Sheep. After standing motionless for a second or two, she sprang upward and walked along Sheep's side to where Alli's long thin nose lay on Sheep's woolly shoulder. She then crossed the nose, hurried forward, and quickly settled herself upon Sheep's cheek. She sat down just in time to see the soap give a quick jerk at one edge and then begin to shake all over. Mrs. Mouse knew what this meant, and she began to shake a little herself—from happy relief.

Sheep had been watching, too, while Mrs. Mouse enjoyed the view from her newly found lookout post. And because Sheep WAS Mrs. Mouse's newly found lookout post, she shared the view with her almost as if they were looking out of one pair of eyes. The thought then came to Sheep that perhaps she and Mrs. Mouse were interfering with Alli's view. This was a horrid thought.

I probably am, she told herself miserably. *I'm probably blocking his vision.*

Of course, if Alli had been asked, he would have told Sheep that she was mistaken. He had never known her to block his vision. When he looked straight ahead, which, naturally, he always did, his nose slanted against Sheep's shoulder and pointed upward so that he looked past her neck and to her head and over—in such a way that a little border of curls framed everything he saw. And Alli found this quite charming. *It is one of the things that makes my location so choice,* he often told himself.

Alli stared at the familiar whitish border upon which Mrs. Mouse seemed to be seated, and began to enjoy himself. *Sheep's little border,* he thought tenderly, a border that swirled and curled and shimmered and gleamed with a soft and pearly light. His thoughts spun joyously with the curls and then stood still, all lined up in a little rhyme. He sang the rhyme out loud, like a song:

"Surely only a churl
  Could object to a curl!"

Good heavens, thought Alli, *I made that up myself! How extraordinary!*

But he had not long to admire his song. He had scarcely finished singing when Mrs. Mouse suddenly leaped away from Sheep's cheek. *Here we go,* Alli told himself. *Things are beginning. Or, rather, they have* BEGUN!

6
Escape!

"Snooch," snuffled Mr. Mouse as his labors on the sticky soap began. "Snooch, sluppity."

Mr. Mouse's sniffles and gasps and wheezes soon became the only sounds to be heard in the Trunk as all attention focused upon his struggles.

His task at the lock-hole is going to be long and hard, thought Teddy Bear. *I hope he makes it.*

All the toys were extremely uncomfortable. They realized that unless Mr. Mouse's task was accomplished by dawn, Mrs. Mouse and all four little ones might be lost.

Time is going by, thought Rebecca nervously. *The night is passing.* From her position in the depths of the Trunk, she could hear little of the agonizing coughs and sneezes and wheezy gasps that now punctuated Mr. Mouse's sniffles and gurgles. He was not stopping to get his breath. He simply gasped and worked on.

Climbing once again to her vantage point on Sheep's cheek, Mrs. Mouse implored her husband, "Do not swallow, my dear! I beg of you, take care not to swallow."

I don't see how he can help it, thought Velvi, *a little bit, anyhow. Oh, how I wish I didn't have to listen!*

The sounds went on and on and did not grow easier. Indeed, they grew worse.

Alli, who was so prone to look at things squarely, told himself: *Things have got to come together soon.*

Cow felt an increasing sense of uneasiness. *Dawn must be almost here,* thought Rebecca.

The tenseness of the whole Trunk seemed to envelop her.

"What hideous noises! Never have there been such noises in our Trunk," murmured Velvi unhappily.

"Never such brave ones," responded Alli.

Is that what brave sounds like? Sheep asked herself. *I always thought it was bugles and drums.*

Suddenly the sounds became quite desperate. Snuffles, sniffles, sneezes, coughs, gurgles, and gasps were happening all at once, and the soap was behaving quite wildly.

Now he's really at it, thought Teddy Bear. "He's certain to burst through or burst trying," he observed with alarm.

Instantly alert, Mrs. Mouse darted away from the lock-hole to the entrance of her nest. The toys heard her voice command in quiet urgency: "Now . . . FORMATION!"

At her words, the little mice tumbled from the nest and skidded to their battle stations. There they pressed tightly against one another, with Slow in front, his toes grabbing the tear in the blue satin that was his battle station, followed by Medium Fast, then Fast, with The Swiftest behind the three, his strong body braced to both push and spring.

Mrs. Mouse rushed back to the lock-hole, where the soap was dancing with incredible liveliness as Mr. Mouse bit, pushed, and butted.

Then it happened.

With a loud smack, the soap shot from the lock-hole past Alli's head and Sheep's shoulder and landed in the Trunk.

At first, the toys wondered what they were seeing.

With water streaming from the end of his nose, and a dreadful soap-bubble garment enveloping him, Mr. Mouse was framed in the lock-hole like an astounding, never-to-be-forgotten portrait.

Even Alli had to stare for a few seconds before being sure that the amazing thing was really Mr. Mouse. Only Mrs. Mouse knew at once that this apparition was he.

"My dear!" whispered Mrs. Mouse. "Magnificent!"

"Glurb!" exclaimed Mr. Mouse in triumph.

"Don't come into the Trunk, my dear,"

warned Mrs. Mouse at once. "There's danger here. The children and I are coming out."

For a second, Mr. Mouse peered searchingly into his wife's wide, frightened eyes, and then abruptly his head descended from the lock-hole, leaving iridescent, gently sailing bubbles in his stead.

Mrs. Mouse gazed at the empty lock-hole for a moment as though bewitched. Then she turned toward her children, who waited, taut as four drawn bows—and as ready.

"CHARGE!" Her voice rang with authority.

Escape, please escape, thought Velvi fervently. She held the words in her mind as hard as she possibly could, as if the pressure of her thoughts might help the mice get away.

Propelled by the power of The Swiftest, with their heads thrust forward and their noses quivering, the four mice shot through the lock-hole as if a single arrowhead.

"Bravo!" shouted Teddy.

The toys could hear the mice streaking across the attic floor. Even Slow moved faster than he ever had before and, perhaps, ever would. *I'm keeping up,* he thought, and his heart beat even faster.

The pale and milky light of dawn beamed through the empty lock-hole and bathed Mrs. Mouse in its tender rays as she watched her children disappear into the safety of the mouse-hole in the wall. With a sigh of relief, she drew herself away from the lock-hole and turned to face the Trunk and its occupants—the toys, the scattered scraps and rags and worn-out clothes, the box of pins, and the mothballs.

Her eyes sent a silent message of good-bye to her friends in the Trunk with a look of such warmth, such fondness, that each in the Trunk felt his own private farewell, and each felt as though embraced.

Then she was gone.

All the toys heard the little smack as she landed in Mr. Mouse's soapy arms and the quick whispering sound as the two skimmed across the attic floor to join their children in the recesses of the passage in the wall.

And now, once again, the lock-hole was its accustomed self—a listening hole, a window to the world. The soft gray light sifted through and fell on Sheep's curls and illumined Alli's nose with beaming light. For a few seconds there was silence in the Trunk.

Then, softly at first, the music of the Trunk sounded once more. The straight pins tinkled sweetly in their box. The mothballs commenced to hum.

"Farewell, farewell," sang the scraps and rags and worn-out clothes. Their words were back!

"It's sad to lose those for whom we care
When our Here becomes their There,
But in the memories that we share,
We are together no matter Where."

After the song ended, it was quiet in the Trunk for a very long time.

Then suddenly the silence was broken by the staccato clumping of footsteps on the stairs.

"Aunt Essie and Aunt Maude!" exclaimed Alli from his vantage point. "The time has come."

"Good grief," called Cow, "the beginning of the end."

"No," said White Bunny, "not the beginning of the end . . . the beginning of the Begin-ning . . . the Beginning of the All."

"With the Wonderfuls, I presume," said Cow scornfully.

"Exactly," replied White Bunny.

Now Velvi heard another sound—footsteps,

soft and thumping, heading straight for the Trunk.

"What's that? What's that thing?" Velvi's voice quavered.

"You really should know," Alli informed her. "That is the cat!"

7
Invasion

"Stand aside, Essie. I'm going to open the trunk," ordered Maude.

Instantly, the Trunk was invaded by blazing lights, blaring sounds from the street, and the heavy, threatening thud of Tom landing in its midst.

The cat went to work at once, rooting and pawing his way purposefully toward the fragrant mouse scent deep within the Trunk. Scraps and rags went helter-skelter as he eagerly pursued his search.

"There's no one home," said Alli.

As if he understood, Tom stopped suddenly, crouched, and slowly scrutinized the contents of the Trunk. At the sight of Velvi, his eyes narrowed, and still crouching, he stalked to her side. Carefully and deliberately he sniffed around her head and nose.

"I believe he knows you," called Alli. "He recognizes you're a cat."

"Oh, no," cried Velvi, "he can't. I'm a different kind of cat entirely. I don't do the things he does. I'm velvet. Real cats don't get to be velvet like me."

"I know, little Velvi," said Alli gently. "I was only joking."

"They're all gone," cried Maude. "Tom can't find them. He's given up. Those nasty mice have gotten away. Look, here's the soap I put in the lock-hole, and there's a tiny bit of cheese by this neatly folded damask. It's almost fresh. I'll wager they've gotten into our new round of Edam, Essie."

"It's from Mrs. Mouse's Treasure," said Sheep softly. "It must have broken off when she ate it."

"And look, here's the empty nest," added Maude as she gingerly lifted it out of the Trunk.

Essie took the nest from her, cupping it softly in her hands. "It's still warm," she observed.

"Throw the nasty thing away, Essie," ordered Maude.

"It's so soft," commented Essie as she gently dropped the nest into the trash box beside the Trunk.

"And so empty, thank goodness," added Cow.

"Where do you suppose they went, Maude?" asked Essie.

"They probably went out that rathole in the wall by the stairs. I'll nail a board across it. Obviously, soap doesn't work."

"If you do, they'll be trapped," warned Essie.

"I certainly hope so," snapped Maude.

"Good heavens," cried Cow. "I can't bear to think of that."

"Try not to worry," said White Bunny. "Remember, where I am, near the nest, I could hear

all the family talks. Many a time, Mr. Mouse
has told his family all about the passages beyond
the mousehole.

"In the center, there's a roomy hollowed-out
place, just the right size for a dwelling place
that he called the Mouse House. There's room,
he says, for a nice cozy new nest just the right
size for Mrs. Mouse and the family, and around
the edges plenty of storage space for food. This
mousehole in the attic is only one of many en-
trances and exits all over the house. There's even
one to the outdoors.

"So you see, Cow," he concluded, "there's
no need to worry over their life in the Mouse
House but, rather, to rejoice."

"With that layout, you couldn't ever plug
them up—or corner them with a dozen cats,"
added Alli as Tom began to move again within
the Trunk.

"Thank you, White Bunny, for recalling all
that," said Sheep. *And thank you, Alli, for adding
to our comfort,* she added silently.

The toys became more comfortable after Tom,
giving Velvi a final sideways glance, jumped out

of the Trunk; but their discomfort returned as Aunt Maude's bony fingers started rummaging in their midst.

"Let's get all these toys out of here," she said. "That will leave more room for the linens we want to store. We'll keep the pins and rags and old clothes; they'll be good for our mending and quilting. And of course these mothballs should stay," she added as she moved the Trunk's contents around.

"Look what I've found, Essie!" she exclaimed, holding Rebecca aloft.

"Oh, let me see that doll, Maude." Essie peered closely. "It's Rebecca!" she exclaimed. "Be careful with her—she's ever so old. I believe she belonged to old Aunt Tess."

Not OLD Aunt Tess, thought Rebecca indignantly. *Not AUNT Tess at all. She was dear little Tessie. I was her first doll. I was her beloved. What wonderful times we had together!*

"Remember the day Aunt Tess brought this doll—her doll—as a present to the Child?" continued Aunt Essie. "Remember how excited She was? She ran upstairs and brought Her doll bed down to the parlor and started undressing the doll. What trouble She had with the tiny, tiny buttons." Aunt Essie smiled in remembrance.

Aunt Maude smiled, too. "I remember Aunt Tess warned Her to be very careful—that Rebecca's clothes were very old and fragile—and the Child immediately wanted to know what 'fragile' meant."

"And She WAS careful—very careful," observed Aunt Essie. "See what good care Rebecca has had. Even though her clothes are yellowed, there's not a split or tear."

Well, Rebecca was right, thought Cow. *She's been right all along. She's been around ever so much longer than the rest of us. She is a real* ANTIQUE.

"Here, put Rebecca over on that old rocker," directed Maude as she carefully handed the doll to Essie. "Of course we want to save HER.

"I suppose YOU know the names of all these others as well," Maude said as, one by one, she dug them out of the Trunk and passed them over to Essie.

"Of course I do. Don't you?"

"Of course I don't," answered Maude sharply. "They were just playthings."

"But not to Her," insisted Essie.

Well, at least Aunt Maude knew MY *name,* thought Rebecca. *She can't be blamed if she doesn't know the others. She never ever knew.*

"We could put Rebecca on the whatnot," said Maude. "She could sit on one of those doilies we were going to stow away. Really, I believe she could be quite a little conversation piece," she concluded.

"That would certainly be a change," observed Alli wryly. "In my remembrance, Rebecca's been the one to MAKE conversation—over and over and piece by piece."

"Would you like to go sit on a doily?" questioned Teddy in horror.

"What about the rest of us?" Velvi asked fearfully. "I'm called Velvi because I'm velvet. Am I going to be saved?"

"I don't think I'd ask," suggested Alli.

"I guess we should throw the others away," said Maude, as if in response to Velvi's question.

"Oh, my word," groaned Cow, "throw away?"

"Away!" cried Teddy Bear joyously. "Where is 'away'? It sounds exciting!"

"Why don't we put these others in this paper sack and take them down to the kitchen?" suggested Aunt Essie. "Then we can decide."

"Why the kitchen, Alli?" asked Sheep.

"Well, think, and you can guess," said Cow. "Where does the back door lead?"

"It leads OUT!" cried Teddy Bear from upside down in Aunt Essie's grasp.

White Bunny had gone into the grocery bag first, and now Teddy Bear fell on top of him. Cow was pushed in on top of Teddy. Sheep felt a moment of terror as Aunt Maude tried to separate her curls from Alli's ragged nose.

"What's the use?" Aunt Maude finally asked in exasperation. "They're hopelessly tangled. Let's leave them as is."

Sheep felt a surge of relief as she and Alli fell together into the sack. Velvi was placed on top of all with her head just peeking out of the sack.

Suddenly a sound, a wonderful sound, rose faintly from the Trunk. The scraps, the rags, and the worn-out clothes were singing words again, sweetly and gently. More than this, they were all singing together in chorus and in broad daylight. Unheard of! The toys strained to catch their song.

> "Our little love has already flown,
> But we sing again though she be gone.
> We send our song to each of you,
> And all we sing is good and true.
> Of luck and love our song doth tell
> And brings to you all a fond farewell."

"Farewell," echoed Alli from within the sack.

"Mrs. Mouse was their 'little love,' " explained Velvi.

"But the song was ours," said Cow. "They said so."

"We were serenaded," said Teddy Bear, "and that is quite an honor."

"We were sung a farewell," whispered Sheep.

"I'll take Rebecca down to the whatnot now, Essie," said Aunt Maude, picking up the doll.

"Farewell, my friends. There's hardly time for a proper farewell, everything's so rushed and hurried," chattered Rebecca as Aunt Maude moved toward the attic steps.

"Farewell, my friends. I shall truly miss you; but of course you couldn't expect to share my place of honor on the Whatnot as a Conversation Piece. We all know I'm an ANTIQUE. You're old, but not that old," she added cheerfully.

"I'm really glad she's going to be happy," commented Sheep. "She and that doily can have endless conversations, and of course, there'll be other knickknacks to share memories of the past with her—especially the china figurines. Won't she like that!"

How sweet of Sheep, thought Alli tenderly.

"Farewell once more." Rebecca's voice floated faintly from below. Aunt Essie followed behind with her grocery sack full of toys.

"This is going to be an important trip," Velvi said in a quivering voice. "I'm about to catch a glimpse of myself, since I went in the bag last."

At her words, the toys recalled the mirror in the hall at the foot of the attic stairs. How often they had looked at themselves as She carried them down to play outside under the old elm tree! But they felt uneasy for Velvi.

"Her tail's hanging by three threads," whispered Sheep to Alli. "One ear is gone. What if she sees how dull and worn her velvet self really is?"

"You don't have to worry about what Velvi sees," whispered Alli. "Velvi will see what she wants to see."

Hurry past the mirror, prayed Sheep silently.

In a few seconds, they were at the bottom of the stairs. As Aunt Essie maneuvered to get both her portly body and the sack piled high with toys through the narrow doorway, her heel caught on the very last step. Leaning forward to catch her balance, she gave Velvi just time to see a passing reflection of black poking out of a brown bag.

"It's really true," cried Velvi happily. "I am a vision of velvet—of beautiful black velvet."

I needn't have worried, thought Sheep. *Alli was right like he always is. He's so smart!*

With slow, careful steps, Aunt Essie made her way down a second flight of stairs and into the kitchen, placing the sack on the kitchen table. As she unloaded it, she carried each of the toys one by one—except for Alli and Sheep, who of necessity went two by two—and leaned them in a row against the baseboard beneath the kitchen window. Then she stepped back to look at them once more.

"I hope we pass inspection," murmured Cow.

"What if we don't?" asked Velvi anxiously.

"What on earth are you doing now, Essie, with those toys spread all over the kitchen floor?" exclaimed Maude as she walked into the room.

"I thought we ought to look them over," answered Essie. Aunt Maude nodded in agreement.

"I guess you're right, Essie. One of these days, the Child is going to come looking for some of Her favorite toys—like this cow, disreputable as she is, and this worn-out rabbit."

"She called the rabbit White Bunny, " corrected Essie. "She took him everywhere She went. Remember how She brought him to the dining room for meals? White Bunny was special. She told him all Her secrets. What on earth are we going to do with him, Maude?"

Not pausing for an answer, Essie answered her own question. "I think he should be put on the chiffonier in the playroom. There's a lovely view from there through the bay windows over the window seat."

"Do be sure he has a view, Essie," snapped Maude. "But I think you're right. The chiffonier is a good spot. He'll be out of the way, but where he's available if She comes our way again. We'll do it tomorrow."

The playroom! Images of the big, airy room flashed in White Bunny's head: the long wall lined with books . . . the empty shelf where the toys were stored at night . . . the doll bed where Rebecca slept . . . the toy table and chairs where She held her tea parties. *How wonderful to be put back there!* thought White Bunny. *The room's full of happy memories of Her.*

"But what about Cow?" asked Aunt Essie. "She was a favorite, too."

"We're making that room into our quilting room, Essie. We can't fill it with a lot of old toys," said Aunt Maude firmly. "Tomorrow morning we'll take the rest of the toys out early enough for the garbage collection."

"Do you really think we should send them to the dump? I wish we wouldn't," protested Essie.

"Why not?" questioned Maude. "They have to go somewhere. You're getting too old for play-things, Essie. They've got to go."

Aunt Essie gave the toys a last kindly look

over her shoulder as she followed Aunt Maude from the room.

"I'm glad we've got a night to visit with each other," said Sheep softly, breaking the stunned silence that had suddenly settled on the kitchen.

8
Night in the Kitchen

"Did you hear what Aunt Maude called me?" asked Cow gloomily. "She called me disreputable! I never expected to be a Treasure or an Antique, but never before has anyone suggested that I'm disreputable." Her voice broke.

"Well, think about what Aunt Maude also said," put in White Bunny. "I believe she called you a favorite."

"That certainly sounds a lot better," said Cow. "Thank you, White Bunny. But then," she added sourly, "why aren't *I* going back to the playroom, too?"

"Oh, White Bunny," said Sheep, "I'm so happy for you."

"So am I," said Alli.

"We all are," said Teddy.

"Even if some of us ARE disreputable," said Cow crossly.

Poor old Cow, Velvi was thinking. *I had forgotten you were so unbecoming. Why, you are almost coming apart! Perhaps it will take your mind off yourself if we talk about* ME.

"Tell me about MY looks, please, Cow," she said aloud. "I caught a glimpse of myself in the hall mirror on the way down. I looked dark and mysterious—but I had only a glimpse."

Cow and Velvi had often talked to one another in the Trunk, but they had been hidden from each other's view by scraps and rags. Now, for the first time in a long, long time, they saw each other face to face.

Poor little thing, thought Cow. *I mustn't let her know how she really looks. It's a good thing she didn't ask me about her ears—one of them has fallen off—or her tail, which is hanging by three threads, or her seams, which are splitting.*

"Why, you are very black, Velvi," said Cow gently, "and you are the most velvet thing I ever saw."

"Mysterious, too?" asked Velvi.

"Oh, VERY! Oh, very much so," said Cow kindly.

"For goodness' sake," cried Teddy Bear, "we've got a lot more important things to think about than what we look like. Think about to-morrow morning and us out in the wide, waiting world!"

"And the garbage man," added Velvi nervously. "Think about how lucky Rebecca is. The lucky thing, she's going to be all dressed up! Why, she'll be ALWAYS dressed up."

"And she's going to see everything! And hear everything!" interrupted Teddy Bear excitedly.

"She'll be with People all the time. She'll be a Great Pleasure to them. Oh, how I'd like to be a Great Pleasure," wished Sheep aloud.

Sweet little Sheep, you always are, thought Alli.

"She's probably sitting on that Whatnot right

now. Right on that doily she admired so much," continued Velvi. Then she paused a long pause.

"Do you know what that means?" she cried. "It means that Rebecca's in her Wonderful!"

"So it does!" exclaimed Teddy. "Something Wonderful HAS happened. It's a beginning. Things have started to roll."

"My Wonderful's with me now," Alli announced.

"Why, for heaven's sake?" cried Velvi.

"Because this is a good place," said Alli, enjoying the comfort of Sheep's cheek. *As a matter of fact, this is my perfect home,* he added to himself as he looked at Sheep's dear, thin, worn-out curls.

"My Wonderful's with me now," Alli repeated.

Now, what in the world did he mean by that? wondered Sheep. *He's so hard to understand sometimes.* She looked at Alli and noted with admiration that an airy ball of dust had settled on his back. *Like a lovely little cloud,* thought Sheep.

"I like it here, too," said Teddy Bear. "I like it because I'm—"

"You don't have to finish," Cow interrupted. "We know! You like it because you're out—

out of the Trunk. Well, you're out, all right. You're out lying on a kitchen floor awaiting a garbage man in the morning. I think you're out of your head," shouted Cow.

"I'm out in the big wide world," said Teddy Bear happily, "where anything can happen."

"Now you're getting me upset again, Cow," said Velvi. "I don't want to think about a garbage man. It scares me."

"Well, just wait, Velvi," said White Bunny. "You have to let things cook, and then you have to get ready."

"How can you tell when it's ready time?" asked Velvi.

"It's a feeling, Velvi," said White Bunny. "Like the feeling you get the last minute before a surprise. Be ready. Don't let your Wonderful go by and not even see it."

"Well, I don't know what to think," said Velvi miserably.

"This is just plain ridiculous," said Cow. "Am I supposed to find a Wonderful sitting on a kitchen floor?"

"Why not?" asked Alli. "Just wait. That's what White Bunny is saying to you."

"Wait for WHAT?" asked Velvi.

There was no answer, and for some time silence enveloped the kitchen.

Light from a rising half-full moon shone through the kitchen window, past the toys, casting shadowy shapes on the kitchen floor.

"It's moonlight! I'd forgotten moonlight," exclaimed Teddy Bear.

"It's so soft," observed Sheep finally.

But not so soft as you, thought Alli.

"Wouldn't it be comforting to have the mothballs humming, the pins tinkling, and the rags singing?" asked Sheep. "What did the words say in the song they sang after Mr. and Mrs. Mouse left?" she asked dreamily.

"It was about our Here becoming their There," explained Alli. "That's what's going to happen tomorrow."

"Yes, that's when your Here becomes my There," observed White Bunny. "We'll just have to remember the music, the words, and how we were."

"Having is better than remembering," objected Alli.

"Sometimes you have to remember in order

to have," answered White Bunny. "Isn't that so, Velvi?"

There was no reply from Velvi.

"Is something the matter, Velvi?" asked Alli.

"I think I know what's wrong," Cow whispered. "Ever since the moon came up, Velvi has been able to see her reflection in the glass part of the oven door. She can see her whole self from head to foot. She's been staring, silently staring, and she's stopped being Velvi."

"I agree," said White Bunny. "Something is really going on with Velvi. She's TOO quiet."

"She's like a rock," said Teddy. "Do you suppose she is PETRIFIED?"

"Of course not," cried Cow indignantly. "Don't you understand ANYTHING? It's the shock. The shock of SEEING."

"It showed her," Alli said. "The surprise is too much."

"Do you suppose she always suspected a bit?" asked Sheep. "Once in a while? Oh, poor little Velvi."

Now Velvi's voice was heard, faint, and not like any Velvi voice heard before.

"Now I know just what I really look like." It was half sob, half moan.

"Help her, Alli," whispered Sheep softly.

Sheep's voice, filled with gentleness as she appealed to him in a time of need, strongly affected Alli.

"Velvi?" called Alli.

Velvi was silent.

He tried again. "Velvi! VELVI!"

"We all know her name," observed Cow crossly.

That's IT, thought Alli happily. *Now I've got it!*

He spoke gently to Velvi, and as if he truly meant what he was saying. He thought he probably *did* mean it—very nearly, anyway.

"Velvi," said Alli again to the strangely silent Velvi. "Nobody could ever forget your name. It is so YOU. And you are so NAMELY. That is, you are so velvet, Velvi."

Velvi finally spoke. "Do you really think so?" she asked weakly.

"Oh, yes," Alli replied quickly, "so much so."

"Yes, but my seam is splitting," said Velvi faintly, and in a whisper she added: "I have only one ear."

"But you ARE still—still velvet," insisted Alli. "Isn't that true, White Bunny?"

"Of course," White Bunny concurred.

"Do you really think so?" Velvi's voice was a little stronger. Then it dropped again. "But my tail is coming off."

"It can be fixed," Sheep interjected.

"Of course it can," echoed Cow.

"Oh, thank you," murmured Velvi. "Maybe things will be all right. Maybe I could be fixed up."

"Of course you could," Alli assured her.

It's like we're doing it together, he thought. *We're mending Velvi right now. All of us.*

"Thank you, Alli. Thank you all so much," said Velvi in a voice that was almost normal.

"Let's not be so polite," cried Teddy. "It's such a bore."

"I wouldn't worry about that," said Cow. "I'm sure the crisis has blown over already."

"Yes," said Velvi suddenly in her natural voice. "What you say is true, Alli. I have always been very velvet, and I still am."

"We've got Velvi back," said Teddy Bear.

"With all the trimmings," added Alli.

9
Dispersion

"It's the crack of dawn," said Aunt Essie in a hurried, worried voice, addressing the toys as she opened the door into the kitchen. "We can't waste a minute. The garbage man will be here soon, and I've decided I want to take you to the dump myself."

She picked up Teddy Bear and laid him in the wicker basket hanging over her arm. On

top of Teddy came Alli and Sheep crowded together so that Alli's face was buried in Sheep's
woolly curls.

"We're more tangled than ever, Alli," observed Sheep in a satisfied voice.

"I can't see a thing, little Sheep," replied Alli.
"Keep me informed."

"Cow's being put in on top of me," Sheep
duly reported. "She looks very unsettled. And
here comes Velvi last of all. She looks scared
to death."

"White Bunny, you're going to be left behind," announced Aunt Essie to the lone figure
left on the kitchen floor. "I'll put you up in
the playroom when I get back."

"Happy days for White Bunny," said Velvi
in a strange voice. "At least HE's not traveling
into the unknown."

"I shall miss you, everyone," called White
Bunny as Aunt Essie opened the outside door.

"Good-bye, White Bunny. . . . Good-bye,"
the toys called in unison.

Velvi just had time to add, "Don't forget us,
White Bunny. We won't ever forget you," before

Aunt Essie stepped out the kitchen door and closed it softly behind her.

"Isn't it great? We're on our way!" shouted Teddy as Aunt Essie started down the driveway.

"We all KNOW we're on our way," said Velvi miserably, "but don't you care where?"

"Aunt Essie will look after us, won't she, Alli?" asked Sheep.

"Of course she will," said Alli, not at all sure this was true.

"I can see through the slats in the basket," exclaimed an excited Teddy. "I can see the old elm tree where the swing used to be. I used to see so much when She would swing high in the sky with me in Her lap. The breeze was so warm. It's warm like that today."

"At least it's summer," observed Cow. "I'm glad it's summer."

As Aunt Essie turned the corner into the road, the scene shifted, and Teddy Bear could no longer see the house and the elm tree—just a dusty winding road ahead.

"Now it's really unknown," said Velvi. "It's all unknown to me."

"And to all of us, happily," added Teddy Bear. "Hurrah!"

"Stop crowing, Teddy," said Cow disagreeably. "Don't say another word."

Now there was no sound but the scraping of Aunt Essie's shoes on the gravel road.

As she reached the dump, Aunt Essie eyed the strange real estate, carefully viewing possible locations for suitable roadside homes. Suddenly one was there—a little bed of bright-green moss surrounded by a circlet of waving wildflowers. A small sandstone ledge of rock overhung the mossy green bed.

"Why, that is made for Sheep and Alli as though it had been planted and grown for them," cried Aunt Essie happily. Lifting Alli and Sheep, she carefully placed them on the soft green couch. She arranged and rearranged them until satisfied that she had the best possible position for them both. Alli's long tin nose was again resting happily against Sheep's shoulder, and her curls again framed his view.

"An excellent choice," said Alli aloud.

"Like a dream come true," murmured Sheep. "What a beautiful place for watching sunrises and sunsets—and showers," she added as a big drop of rain splashed nearby.

Aunt Essie's attention to her task had been so intent that the raindrop came as a real surprise. *We're in for a sudden summer shower,* she thought, and she quickly placed Cow in a tight little place just behind the mossy couch.

"This rock will protect you from the rain. Somehow cowhide doesn't like water after it's off the cow—and you're real cowhide even though you're a toy cow," Essie added. Turning back to her basket, she hurriedly grabbed up Teddy Bear.

"It's going to be pouring down in a minute, and I still have you and Velvi to do!" she exclaimed.

Hastily, she made her way to a little hillock nearby. *This Teddy Bear will want to be here in the open where he can see,* she thought. *He has such a looking-away look in his shiny button eyes.*

Oh, lovely whipping wind and slapping rain, thought Teddy as he was set down on a little rise overlooking a busy road below.

The noises of the highway rose in a continuing symphony wonderful to his ears. *Honk, honk,*

honk; *ah-oo-gah, ah-oo-gah*; and the hum-
humming of tires on the road. *And sometimes I'll
hear fire bells and sirens and whistles,* he thought.
A glorious jumble of sound!

As Teddy exulted in his new abode, Aunt
Essie had grabbed Velvi from the basket and
stuffed her hurriedly into her apron pocket.

"I just can't leave you here in this downpour,
little kitty-cat. You'd be a soggy mass of nothing
by evening," she explained. "I wish I didn't have
to leave the others," she added regretfully as
she scurried down the path from the dump. Aunt
Essie held the empty wicker basket over her head
as protection from the rain, which was now falling in sheets.

"I think she's gone away, Alli," said Sheep.
"I think we're alone."

"I think so, too," said Cow from behind her,
"except for ourselves, and hundreds of ants and
bees and dragonflies. I could go on and on,"
she added.

"I'm sure you could," Alli agreed, "but perhaps
this is a good stopping place. Indeed, it is—a
wonderful place to stop and stay."

Thank Aunt Essie for that, he thought as he

gazed happily at his own picture of the falling rain, which was framed by Sheep's tight, wet curls. The wet lavender flowers were slapping against Sheep's cheeks, and the mossy couch grew greener under the pelting rain.

I wonder if I could tell her how lovely she looks with her curls all tight from the dampness, Alli silently asked himself.

Oh, what a privilege to see you, Alli, all washed and gleaming with wetness, thought Sheep. *What a privilege to be right here. I wonder if I should tell you.*

But neither spoke a word aloud.

10
The Letter

By the time Aunt Essie reached home, the summer downpour had ended, but a stormy Aunt Maude met her at the door.

"Where on earth have you been all morning, Essie? I've been waiting for you forever. How did you get so wet?"

"I've been all along the edge of the dump," explained Aunt Essie defensively. "The storm caught me by surprise while I was finding suitable locations for each of the toys."

"I thought the trash man was to tend to that," said Maude.

"But Maude, I couldn't let that happen. They would have been under piles of heaven knows what. As it is, they're each in a pleasant location."

"Well, I see you brought one of them back," noted Maude as she spied a shiny black tail dangling from her sister's pocket.

"I couldn't leave Velvi to disintegrate in the rain—" began Aunt Essie, but Aunt Maude immediately interrupted her.

"Well, Essie, most people would agree you're a very peculiar person, but this time it looks as if your oddness is going to pay off. I've got a very interesting letter to read to you. It came in the morning mail for both of us. That's why I was so anxious for you to come home. Let's go upstairs and get you out of your wet clothes, and then we'll read the letter together in the playroom. It's an appropriate place, as you'll see," she concluded.

"We might as well take White Bunny as we

go," said Essie, scooping him up from his abandonment on the kitchen floor. He was hurriedly placed on the chiffonier in the playroom before Aunt Essie disappeared to change into dry clothes.

In a matter of minutes she returned, cradling Velvi in her arms, and settled herself beside Maude on the window seat so they could share the contents of the letter.

" 'Dear Aunts,' " read Maude aloud, " 'It fills me up with happiness to think of coming, at long last, for a visit with you two. So many happy memories come to mind.' "

"Oh, Maude, how wonderful it will be to see Her again, all grown up!" exclaimed Essie.

Maude nodded in agreement and continued: " 'One of the things I look forward to most is to visit once more with all my beloved toys. I haven't seen them since that day I left for boarding school so long ago. There were seven of them, and I remember them, every one—Cow, Sheep, Alli, little black Velvi, Rebecca, Teddy Bear, and, of course, my beloved White Bunny. The playroom is full of happy rememberings.

They were my friends, my playmates, my world. . . .' "

White Bunny felt a surge of joy. Oh, indeed, it was the happiest of circumstances that She should be coming into his life again!

"Oh, Maude, when does She say She's coming?" interrupted Essie again.

"Right away. She's coming tomorrow," replied Maude. "There's a lot to do before then, and we've just got to have all the toys back. Do you remember where they are at the dump?"

"Of course I do," Essie assured her. "I selected their places. I know exactly where they are. I'll go get them as soon as you finish the letter."

Maude, skimming over the letter, found her place and read on: " 'I've decided to take all the toys back to college with me, for my roommate and I have agreed to decorate our room with all our favorite old playthings. We both want to have them for keepsakes to someday hand down to our children and our children's children. Isn't that a wonderful thought? I think the toys will be as happy as I with that arrangement.' "

"I wonder if She'd have thought the dump a happy arrangement," said Essie darkly.

"We may have acted precipitately, Essie," admitted Maude as she rose to go. Essie rose, too, but stopped on her way out to shift White Bunny on the chiffonier to more squarely face the windows across the room.

"That's better," she pronounced.

"Take Velvi with you, Maude," Essie directed as she left the room. "I'm going to get a needle and thread so you can mend Velvi while I'm at the dump."

Maude picked Velvi up and looked her over carefully. "She does need mending, all right. Her tail is hanging by three threads, and her seams are all splitting."

I do hope Aunt Essie finds the other toys, thought White Bunny. *I hope she finds them all. They'll be so glad to see Her again.* He was happy to share Her love with all the toys, for he had never felt an instant's doubt about Her special devotion to him.

The sun was now streaming through the windows of the playroom. The white-organdy curtains that framed the bay windows were stirring slightly in a freshening breeze. They drew White Bunny's attention, and, looking out, he could see Aunt Essie, wicker basket on her arm, heading down the drive. *Off to collect the toys,* he observed with satisfaction.

Aunt Maude is collecting, too, thought White Bunny a few minutes later when she entered the playroom carrying a stack of starched doilies in her hands and something cradled in her arms. She headed for the small mahogany doll bed that extended from the wall near the window seat.

As Aunt Maude's back was toward him, White Bunny could not quite see what she was doing, but when she stepped aside, there was Rebecca reclining regally atop the newly laundered doilies.

"She's taken me from my new, dear Whatnot friends!" exclaimed Rebecca without pausing for a hello as she saw White Bunny across the room.

"Do you like the Whatnot, Rebecca?" inquired White Bunny politely.

"Of course, W.B. I'm with Antiques there, you know. But I must say I've missed you all. Why are you here by yourself? Where are the others?"

"Just wait, Rebecca. You'll find out."

"That's what you always have said, White Bunny: Wait . . . wait."

"Because it's true, Rebecca. Wait and you'll see. . . ."

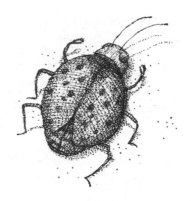

11
Adventures at the Dump

Aunt Essie was limping when she returned from the dump, but she had a satisfied smile on her face and a full basket on her arm.

"All done, Maude—successfully, I might add," she called as she slowly climbed the stairs carrying her basket of toys.

"I see Maude's brought Rebecca in," she observed as she entered the playroom. "Well, I'll put these toys in place, too—if only my poor legs hold out."

Alli and Sheep were laid together on one chair of the Child's table set, and Cow was placed in the opposite chair, her chin resting on the tabletop, looking directly at Alli and Sheep. Aunt Essie placed Teddy on the chiffonier beside White Bunny. There he would have an excellent view out the bay windows.

"What a spot!" Teddy exclaimed happily. "I can see the world."

"Do you see me down here, Teddy Bear?" called Rebecca after Aunt Essie had left the room. "I'm here in my BOO-DWAH—that's French, you know. I learned it from a Dresden figurine on the Whatnot."

"Thank you so much, Rebecca," said Alli in a mock drawl. "It's educational to all of us, I'm sure. We'll try to remember it. Meanwhile, 'pleasant dreams'—that's in English, you know."

How clever Alli is, thought Sheep. *He knows languages.*

"Where's Velvi?" Rebecca continued. "I know she'd like to see my BOO-DWAH. Why isn't she with you?"

"She's with Aunt Maude," explained White Bunny. "Aunt Maude is fixing her up good as new."

"I think Teddy Bear could stand a bit of fixing, too," observed Rebecca. "His face is dirty. Where on earth have you all been?"

"At the dump," retorted Teddy.

"The dump!" exclaimed Rebecca, horrified.

"Yes, and it was a wonderful adventure," said Teddy Bear. "There were exciting noises, like thunder and rain and wind, and it was glorious until the wind blew me over—nose down in the mud. I could no longer see, only hear. I would have been miserable, but I was suddenly struck by some tremendous missile.

"In the most considerate way, the missile began to speak to me, and, as I remember, this is what he said: 'From your prone position you cannot see me; so I'll identify myself. I am a beetle—round in shape and about the size of a plum. My highly polished enamel coat is in black and white stripes, and my pincers and legs are a dark-bright orange.' "

By now, Teddy Bear had the attention of all the toys.

"Then," continued Teddy, "with manners most elegant, he asked if he might hang on to me.

" 'Of course,' I answered instantly, and told the beetle I would be delighted with his company. As the wind buffeted him about, he moved from place to place, clinging to my body, and he explained that he had just come out from his home and was blown there by the storm.

" 'Where did you come out from?' I asked him.

" 'Out from my present dwelling,' he replied, 'an ideal situation' "—Teddy Bear paused for effect—" 'a place called the Mouse House.'

"I simply yelled in amazement," Teddy Bear said. " 'Do you mean Mrs. Mouse and her children—and Mr. Mouse? Do you stay at their home?'

" 'I do call the Mouse House my home, at this time,' he replied, 'and I'm happy to be able to say that I'm of great assistance to Mr. Mouse in gathering his feasts. My wings are of particular help in reaching high places, and I've been able to save Mr. Mouse from many a weary time.'

"Was he astounded," Teddy exclaimed,

"when I declared that I had lived in a Trunk in the attic of the very same house!

"Then he told me he had just been to that very same Trunk, and he gave me news of the pins and scraps and rags and worn-out clothes and mothballs and, in particular, of the old pillowcase, of whom he is quite fond.

"And then he said to me, 'The wind seems to have died down, and I'd like to see you face to face. If there is no objection, I'll walk around your nose, and our eyes will be on the same level.' He walked slowly and laboriously around my nose, and our eyes met in immediate recognition of one another. I saw at once the magnificence of my guest. His description of himself scarcely did him justice. He was, by far, the most magnificent insect I've ever seen.

"It was at this point," Teddy Bear continued, "that Aunt Essie arrived to pick me up. The beetle stood high on his prickly legs in preparation for flight, thanked me for being unspeakably useful, and promised to carry messages back to our old friends." Teddy Bear paused for breath.

"I had neither so dramatic nor quite so pleasant an encounter with insects, myself," interposed

Alli. "Aunt Essie had selected a very appealing spot for Sheep and me, but she didn't reckon on ants. How could she know I was in their roadbed? I had been situated only a few minutes before a line of hundreds of them rushed across my body from left to right, and a similar line came back the other way. They continued on and on even through the rain. I became no more than a highway!"

"My guests were bees," said Sheep. "I was visited by bees and more bees. They seemed to mistake my curls for little white flowers, and each had to sit and investigate until realizing her mistake. I can still hear their buzzing."

"Well, all I got were thoughts of home," said Cow. "I'm a homebody; my body belongs at home."

"And which of all places may that be?" inquired Alli. "The old Trunk?"

"Well, the Trunk was just-the-samey," murmured Cow. "It was sweetly just-the-samey and very much so—today, tomorrow, and yesterday."

"Let's not forget the spacious comfort of this playroom," persisted Alli. "With its memories of Her. Did you not tell us THAT was your Wonderful?"

"True, oh, true," sighed Cow. "And yet I loved the Trunk, too. Oh, White Bunny, please, please, tell me where my home is. Where should I long to be?"

"Just watch and wait, Cow," comforted White Bunny. "You will know it. Just watch and wait."

"Well, Cow," said Teddy Bear in tones more measured than the toys had ever heard him use, "I guess I understand a little. It's something I learned at the dump. A roof over one's head is not to be despised. My inside stuffing is still damp from that storm."

"So much for beetles, bees, and ants," said Alli dryly, "and, speaking of home, do you know why we've been brought back here, White Bunny?"

"Indeed I do, Alli," responded White Bunny. "I have NEWS. SHE is coming back. SHE is coming to see us!"

12
Velvi's Reappearance

The toys had scarcely absorbed White Bunny's words and poured out expressions of joy at his news when the playroom door opened and in walked the two aunts, who proceeded directly to the window seat.

"Look, they've brought in Velvi," exclaimed Cow, straining to make Velvi out in the graying twilight that now enveloped the room. "Just look at her! She's all spruced up. Her tail is tight, her seams don't show, and she has TWO ears."

"Indeed, I have," called Velvi happily from the window seat, where she lay curled up between Aunt Maude and Aunt Essie. "Hello, everybody! I'm so glad to see you!"

"We're glad you're here, Velvi," called Sheep.

"Yes, indeed," added Rebecca. "You look perfectly beautiful."

"Why, thank you, Rebecca," said Velvi in a pleased voice.

"In my world," muttered Alli, "there's but one who is perfectly beautiful."

There he goes, being mysterious again, thought Sheep.

The toys were so involved with Velvi's appearance, they scarcely noticed the playroom door closing softly as both aunts quietly left.

"Aunt Maude sure did a good job on you, Velvi," continued Cow.

"She did, didn't she?" Velvi was almost purring. "Oh, by the way, have you heard the news—"

"—that She is coming back?" interrupted

Teddy Bear. "Yes, White Bunny just told us. How did you know, Velvi?"

"The aunts could talk of nothing else as they put the finishing touches on me," explained Velvi. "They were making plans for Her visit."

"I hope they leave Her time for us," mumbled Cow.

"That's high on their list, Cow," assured Velvi.

"Well, I tell you what's on my list," interrupted Alli. "A little nighttime quiet, if you please. I need time to think."

"We all do," agreed White Bunny, and silence filled the room.

13
The End and the Beginning

"I'm bored with waiting. . . . She's never com-ing," complained Velvi for the tenth time. "Let's play the Sound game again."

"I don't think there're any more sounds left—but I can make a new rule," said Rebecca.

For a while, the toys had enjoyed themselves, listening to all the bustle going on down below and figuring out what each sound meant. They had added smells to the game when the aunts busied themselves in the kitchen.

Teddy Bear heard the grocer's truck before the rest, but White Bunny was the first to hear a mockingbird singing in the old elm tree and had barely been beaten out by Teddy Bear when a robin gave its chirp. Even Alli had joined in and claimed the whine of the vacuum cleaner for his own. Sheep declared she was just too slow for the game, and Velvi had participated only by cheering the players on.

"What's the new rule, Rebecca?" inquired Velvi.

"The new rule is that the only winner is the one who hears Her arrive," declared Rebecca.

"Then I'm it!" shouted Teddy. "I hear a car." And indeed, they all were now able to hear car tires crunching over the gravel drive.

The aunts, too, had heard the car arrive. The toys could hear their footsteps hurrying down the hall, the front door swinging open on its heavy hinges, followed by squeals of happy hellos and my-just-look-how-you've-grown exclamations from the aunts.

"I can hear HER!" shouted Teddy. "She sounds exactly like Herself."

"Don't shout, Teddy. We want to hear, too," said Velvi; but the chattering voices were now hardly audible as Aunt Maude and Aunt Essie led their guest to the parlor.

"They'll be talking for ages, discussing all the family stories they've saved up for each other," said Rebecca in her most I'll-tell-you-how-it-is tone. And she proved right.

"I hope She comes up here soon," said White Bunny after a while. "I can hardly wait!"

"You won't have to," interrupted Teddy Bear. "I believe I hear Her coming—She's coming up the stairs."

Rebecca and Velvi were so situated that they could see Her pausing in the doorway and looking tenderly from toy to toy; then She was inside the room, standing in their midst, and Velvi received the first hug. But She did not neglect a one of them. This time each toy received a long, leisurely embrace.

She was still with the toys when Aunt Maude appeared in the playroom doorway a half hour or so later.

"Dinner is almost ready, my dear," she announced. "Your Aunt Essie is frying the green tomatoes right now. Don't you smell them cooking?''

"Indeed I do," her niece replied. "The delicious smells have made me so hungry that Cow and I just had a tea party together. I hope I have room left for dinner," She teased.

"You know, my dear, for the life of me I could never understand what you see in Cow," blurted Aunt Maude. "She always seemed most unattractive to me. Can you explain your caring?''

"It's difficult to explain, Aunt Maude," She replied. "Don't you see that Cow is a real personage? I couldn't help loving her. Can't you see what beautiful brown eyes she has? I love to look in her eyes, and when I do, there is such love returned to me."

A most wonderful sweep of emotion came over Cow. *Who ever had spoken thus of her before? Who ever had acknowledged her love?*

Overcome, Cow was scarcely aware when she was placed beside White Bunny and Teddy, and the aunt and niece quickly and quietly left the room.

Rebecca spoke first. "This is the best reunion that ever there was," she pronounced.

A chorus of agreement immediately followed her words. "And I haven't missed the Whatnot a single time," she added.

"It is indeed wonderful to have Her with us," said White Bunny. "And it is wonderful that not one of us was lost when we got separated. Again we are seven."

How can I be seven? puzzled Sheep. "I'm only one. I can't be more than one." Without meaning to, she had spoken out loud. "I push my feelings this way and that way, and it always turns out the same. I'm nobody but ME."

"This is as it should be, Sheep," comforted Alli. "You can't be more than one!" He paused and added slyly, "But one and one make two, you know."

There he goes, being mysterious again, thought Sheep.

"Well," Rebecca announced. "I intend to spend a lovely evening talking with my best friends—my beloved doilies—on whom I now rest. We'll take turns telling stories about the long ago, which we so sweetly remember."

"She's coming back up here again tomorrow," Teddy informed White Bunny. "I know because

She said She wants to clean my face before we leave home."

All this time, Cow had not spoken a word. Suddenly she almost shouted.

"Oh, for heaven's sake! Talk about home! I'm home now."

"Would you still feel at home at a college?" queried White Bunny.

"I'm home anywhere She is, White Bunny," Cow replied immediately with great dignity. "I know that now."

"What's this about college, White Bunny?" asked Alli sharply. "Have you told us everything you know?"

What is this college thing? thought Velvi. *I would have told them this news, but I didn't know what it meant.*

"Almost, Alli," responded White Bunny. "Everything has happened so very fast. But it's true: We're off to college tomorrow."

"How nice for you, White Bunny. I know you're happy," said Sheep warmly.

Dear, generous little Sheep, thought Alli.

"She's always loved you very much," observed Rebecca. "I'm not surprised that She's taking you . . . and She must be taking Teddy Bear also," she added a bit crossly.

"She loves us ALL," corrected White Bunny, "and She's taking us ALL. She wants us ALL with Her forever and ever."

"That's right," said Velvi importantly. "That's what Her letter said. I heard it, too.

"I'm ready for this adventure," she added. "I'm not afraid anymore—not since I got all fixed up." *But I wish I knew what is college,* she thought silently.

"The waiting is over," White Bunny continued solemnly. "This is the beginning of a new beginning. The Wonderfuls are ready for all of us, and we each seem ready, too."

His words were met by a chorus of assents throughout the playroom—and for once Cow agreed.

"Yes, yes indeed, White Bunny. Of course."

Do you suppose I'm a one that makes two? wondered Sheep.